Cinderella
and the
Beanstalk

First published in 2013
by Wayland

Wayland
338 Euston Road
London NW1 3BH

Wayland Australia
Level 17/207 Kent Street
Sydney, NSW 2000

Series Editor: Louise John
Cover design: Emil Dacanay
Design: Lisa Peacock
Consultant: Shirley Bickler

A CIP catalogue record for this book is available from the British Library.

ISBN 9780750268646

Printed in China

Wayland is a division of Hachette Children's Books,
an Hachette UK Company

www.hachette.co.uk

Cinderella
and the
Beanstalk

Written by Hilary Robinson
Illustrated by Simona Sanfilippo

WAYLAND

"Jack! Jack! You idle boy!
We have no food to eat.
Take our cow to market
and sell her for some meat."

"And Cinderella, get to work!
Our dresses are too tight.

"Mend them! Wash them! Press them!
It's the prince's ball tonight!"

"Is your cow for sale, my boy?
She's the finest I have seen.

I don't have any money,
but I'll swap her for this bean."

"This magic bean," the old man said,
"will grow and change your life.

Plant it in your garden and
the prince may find a wife!"

The sisters flew into a rage
and threw the bean outside.

Jack ran into the kitchen
to find a place to hide.

Said Cinders, "Look Jack! Look up there! The beanstalk has grown high.

Let's go and climb it, right away,
and see what's in the sky!"

At the very top they heard a voice
that sang out, "Fee, Fi, Fo!"

A giant godmother waved her wand.
"Off to the ball you go!"

A cloud became a carriage,
and stars, her dress and shawl.

Jack sat in the driving seat
to drive off to the ball.

"But when the clock chimes midnight,
you must leave and hurry back,

for your dress will turn back into rags,
and your shawl become a sack."

21

The prince saw Cinderella and
danced with her all night.

But when the clock struck midnight,
she disappeared from sight.

He found the shoe she'd left behind,
and set off on a ride!

"I'll find the owner of this shoe,
and she shall be my bride!"

The ugly sisters tried to squeeze
their feet into the shoe.

The prince saw Cinderella,
and said, "This shoe belongs to you!"

The ugly sisters went out to climb
the beanstalk, but they found,

that when they got to half-way up...
it toppled to the ground!

The prince and Cinderella
were married the next day.

Jack became the palace chef
and the others ran away!

START READING is a series of highly enjoyable books for beginner readers. **The books have been carefully graded to match the Book Bands widely used in schools.** This enables readers to be sure they choose books that match their own reading ability.

Look out for the Band colour on the book
in our Start Reading logo.

The Bands are:

Pink Band 1A & 1B

Red Band 2

Yellow Band 3

Blue Band 4

Green Band 5

Orange Band 6

Turquoise Band 7

Purple Band 8

Gold Band 9

START READING books can be read independently or shared with an adult. They promote the enjoyment of reading through satisfying stories, plays and non-fiction narratives, which are supporte.d by fun illustrations and photographs.

Hilary Robinson loves jumbling up stories and seeing how they turn out. Her life is a jumbled up lot of fun, too! Hilary writes books for children and produces radio programmes for BBC Radio 2 and, because she really likes doing both, she really feels as if she is living happily ever after!

Simona Sanfilippo loves to draw and paint all kinds of animals and people. She enjoyed reading illustrated fairytales as a child and hopes you will enjoy reading these fairytale jumbles, too!